SQUEAK SAVES THE DAY
and Other Tooley Tales

Also by Zilpha Keatley Snyder

SQUEAK SAVES THE DAY
and Other Tooley Tales

ZILPHA KEATLEY SNYDER

Illustrated by Leslie Morrill

Delacorte Press

Published by
Delacorte Press
The Bantam Doubleday Dell Publishing Group, Inc.
1 Dag Hammarskjold Plaza
New York, New York 10017

Designed by Judith Neuman-Cantor

Delacorte Press is a registered trademark of Dell Publishing, a
division of the Bantam Doubleday Dell Publishing Group, Inc.

Library of Congress Cataloging in Publication Data
Snyder, Zilpha Keatley.
Squeak saves the day and other Tooley tales/by Zilpha Keatley
Snyder; illustrated by Leslie Morrill.
p.   cm.
Contents: Introduction—about the Tiddlers—Squeak saves the day—
Trinket's silver cup—Brindle's visitor—Nipper's little stomper—
Jib and the drumbies—The little yellow quen—A doll for Dimity.
ISBN 0-385-29661-4
[1. Fantasy.]   I. Morrill, Leslie H., ill. II. Title
PZ7.S68522Sq   1988
[E]—dc19   87-31010
CIP
AC

MANUFACTURED IN THE UNITED STATES OF AMERICA

May 1988
10 9 8 7 6 5 4 3 2 1
AG

For small Stompers
with unblurrable eyes

Contents

About the Tiddlers

Far away in a deep forest is a little village called Tiddletown. The people who live there are called Tiddlers, and they are just a little bit magic. They use that little bit of magic to hide themselves from —the STOMPERS.

Jib Tooley is a Tiddler. He lives in a cottage in Tiddletown with his wife, Brindle, and his children, who are called Trinket and Nipper.

Tiddletown is a small place. If you were walking through the village, you could step over fences and jump over houses. If you met a Tiddler man, you could pick him up and carry him with one hand. And if the man had red hair and a round middle, he might be Jib Tooley.

Only you probably won't be in Tiddletown. And you probably won't see Jib Tooley. You won't because you are—a STOMPER.

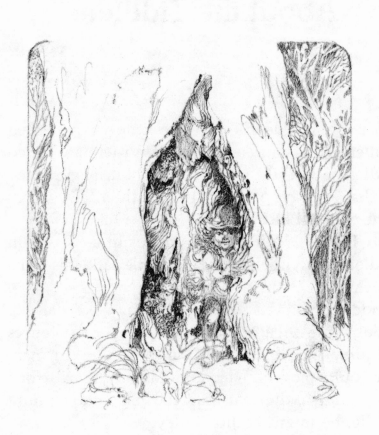

1. Squeak Saves the Day

One fine morning in summer, Jib Tooley went to the window and looked out. It was a beautiful day. All over Tiddletown the sun was warming walls and twinkling windows. Jib took a deep breath. "Let me see," he said. "What shall I do today?"

Brindle Tooley, Jib's wife, was sweeping the floor. "Well," she said, "the grass needs cutting, and the weeds need pulling."

"So they do," Jib said. "So they do. But weeds can wait. And wouldn't a fine fat minnow taste good for supper tonight?"

"True," Brindle said. "Weeds can wait. And around here, they usually do." She swept the last of the dust into a neat pile. "Jib," she said, "could you come here and hold the dustpan?"

But Jib was busy looking for his fishing pole. "Trinket," he shouted. "Come help your mother with the dustpan."

For a moment nothing happened. Then something dashed into the room. The something was a half-grown girl with curly hair and soft blue eyes. "Look!" she said. "Look! I'm a fairy!"

Trinket's skirt was tucked up, and she had flowers in her hair. She ran around the kitchen on tiptoe, flapping her arms. "I'm a fairy!" she said. "I'm flying!"

Brindle was waiting with the broom in one hand and the dustpan in the other. "Well, come down to earth, Miss Fairy, and hold this dustpan."

Trinket flapped across the room. She sat down on the floor and held the dustpan. As Brindle swept up the dust Trinket said, "Didn't I look like a fairy? We're almost fairies, aren't we, Mother? Weren't the Tiddlers almost like fairies in the olden days?"

"So they say," Brindle said. "They say that in the olden days we Tiddlers could fly and do magic. But we can't anymore. At least we can't fly, and we can't do much magic. If we could, I'd just magic this dust right out the door."

"But there still are fairies, aren't there, Mother?" Trinket asked.

"So they say," Brindle said. "But I haven't seen

one lately. Now stop wiggling, and hold that pan still."

Just then the back door of the cottage flew open. A large, fat mouse dashed into the room. Behind the mouse came a boy not much bigger than the mouse.

"Stop!" Brindle called. "Stop that mouse, Nipper, before he . . . Oh, DRAT!"

She swatted at the mouse with her broom and missed. Then she swatted at Nipper and missed him too. Nipper and the mouse dashed out the front door. When they were gone, the dust pile was gone too. The dust was all over Brindle and Trinket.

"Jib," Brindle said, "why don't you take Nipper fishing too? I think he could use a long walk."

Jib smiled. "And you could use some peace and quiet," he said.

"And I could use some peace and quiet too," Trinket said, shaking the dust out of her yellow hair. "And if that mouse gets into my things one more time, I'm going to . . ." She didn't say any more, but at that moment her blue eyes were not so soft.

Nipper stuck his head back in the door. "And

Squeak too," he said. "Could we take Squeak too?"

Very soon Jib and Nipper were on the way to their favorite fishing hole. Jib had fishing poles in one hand and a fish basket in the other. Nipper had a long string in both hands. On the other end of the string was Squeak.

At first, Squeak didn't want to go fishing. He sat down hard and made himself into a fat, round lump. Nipper pulled and pulled, but the round lump stayed where it was. Nipper told him to get up and come along, but Squeak didn't seem to hear. At last Jib had to come back and push. He put down the poles and pushed. He pushed until his face got redder than his hair.

Then Squeak changed his mind. He wanted to go very much. He wanted to go in a hurry. He ran ahead and pulled Nipper after him. Jib grabbed the basket and the poles and came too.

Squeak began to run in a circle. He ran in a circle three times, and then he stopped. When Squeak stopped, Jib and Nipper were sitting in the middle of the path. The string was wrapped around them three times. Squeak was sitting on Jib's lap.

It took a long time to unwrap the string. It was

quite late when Jib and Nipper and Squeak finally got to the stream. Nipper looked at his father. Jib was not looking happy. He sat down and began to fish without saying anything. Nipper tied Squeak to a bush. Then he came back and began to fish too.

Squeak was running around and around the bush. Nipper watched him with one eye and watched his fishing line with the other. Suddenly, something pulled on Nipper's line. A fish was biting. Just then Squeak made a funny noise.

Squeak was lying on the ground. He had run around the bush until the string was used up. Then he had tried to run some more. Now his tongue was hanging out, and his eyes looked much too big. His squeak sounded strange. Nipper dropped his pole and ran to help his mouse.

Nipper picked up Squeak and ran back around the bush. It wasn't easy. Squeak was a fat mouse. Nipper ran around the bush many times. At last Squeak stopped squeaking, and his eyes stopped looking funny.

"It's all right," Nipper called to his father. "I got him loose. Squeak is free now."

"So is your fish," Jib said.

Jib and Nipper went on fishing. They didn't say much. Nipper knew his father was angry. At last Nipper said, "He can't help it, Father. He's only a mouse."

"I know," Jib said. "A mouse is only a mouse, and he is not supposed to be anything else. He is not supposed to be a pet."

"I know," Nipper said. "A dog is a good pet. What I'd really like to have is a dog."

"A DOG!" Jib said. "Why ever would you want a dog?"

"I saw a dog once," Nipper said. "He was with a boy."

"What boy?" Jib asked. "Was he a Tiddler boy?"

"No," Nipper said. "He was a STOMPER boy. I was up in a tree, and I saw them go by down below. They were playing together. The dog was very nice."

"But you are not a STOMPER. And our house is not a STOMPER house. A dog might sit on our house and squash it. A dog might step on you and squash you!"

"But animals don't hurt Tiddler people. Even a wolf or a fox won't hurt one of us."

"Of course," Jib said. "That is because we can blur their eyes. But you can't blur a pet's eyes. And STOMPER animals are too big for Tiddler people." Jib looked at Squeak. "Even a STOMPER mouse like Squeak is too big. And a dog would be impossible. He could hurt you without meaning to."

Nipper looked at his toes. He was not smiling. "If I were a STOMPER boy I could have a dog," he said. "I wish I were a STOMPER boy."

Jib and Nipper looked at each other. They didn't say anything, and they were not smiling. They went on fishing. After a while Jib caught a fish, and then Nipper caught one. But they still didn't say anything to each other. They just put the fish in the basket and went on fishing.

At last Jib said, "You shouldn't have been looking at that STOMPER boy. Even if you were up in a tree, you shouldn't have looked at him. He might have seen you."

"No, he couldn't," Nipper said. "I was blurring his eyes. I know how to blur the eyes of the STOMPERS so they can't see us."

"But it might not have worked," Jib said. "Didn't you know that the magic doesn't always work with little STOMPERS? It always works with the grown-up ones, but sometimes a little one has eyes that can't be blurred. Some little STOMPERS can see Tiddler people."

"I didn't know that," Nipper said. "But, anyway, the boy didn't see me. I was hiding in the tree."

"You were lucky," Jib said. He went on fishing. He didn't say any more to Nipper.

A little later Nipper was fishing quietly when, all at once, something pushed him over and sat on him. The fat brown lump sitting on his back was Squeak. A short string was around his neck. He had chewed it off with his sharp teeth.

"Get off," Nipper said. "Get off me, Squeak. You made me drop my pole." Squeak stayed where he was. At last Nipper pushed him off and climbed down the bank to get his pole.

Just then Jib said, "Hush! Listen! I hear something."

Nipper listened. He could hear footsteps and someone talking. The sounds were getting closer and closer.

"STOMPERS!" Jib said. "They're coming this way."

"We'd better run," Nipper said. "Let's run, Father."

"It's too late to run," Jib said. "They might step on us. Get up here near the tree trunk. We'll blur their eyes. They won't see us."

Jib and Nipper stood quietly near the trunk of the tree. Nipper pulled Squeak next to him by the short piece of string and made him lie down in the grass. Jib and Nipper stood very still, and they both did the magic that blurred the eyes of the STOMPERS.

The footsteps and voices got louder and louder. Then some huge feet in brown boots came around the bend in the path. Above the feet were two legs as big as tree stumps. And above the legs was the rest of a huge man. He was wearing a green coat and had a bushy beard. Behind him came a man in a red coat who was just as big as the first.

"STOMPERS?" Nipper whispered to Jib.

Jib nodded.

"I'd forgotten how big they were," Nipper whispered again.

"Shh!" Jib said.

The four huge legs were very close. The enormous men looked right at Jib and Nipper. But their eyes were blurred. They didn't see anything but a tree trunk. They were almost past when there was another sound. Nipper and Jib looked down the path. Behind the two huge STOMPERS was another one. Only this one was not nearly as big. This one was a STOMPER, all right, but he was a little boy. And with him was a big black dog.

Jib grabbed Nipper's arm. "Look out," he said. "He'll see us."

"What will he do?" Nipper said. "What will the boy do if he sees us?" He looked at his father.

Jib looked frightened. "He might try to catch us," he said.

The boy was getting closer. He was not looking at Jib and Nipper yet. He was looking at the dog. But he would soon be right beside them.

Just then Squeak jumped up. He pulled the string out of Nipper's hand. He gave a squeak and ran right across the path. He ran right in front of the boy and the dog.

The dog saw Squeak. It gave a loud bark and ran after him.

"Hey, Blackie, come back here," the boy called, and he ran after the dog. In a moment they disappeared into the bushes.

Jib and Nipper picked up their poles and the basket of fish. Then they ran across the path and hid in the bushes. They hid for a long time, but nothing more happened. After a while they started to walk back toward the village.

"Squeak saved us," Nipper said.

"It's a true thing you're saying," Jib said. "That he did. Squeak saved the day."

Nipper began to cry. "I wonder what happened to Squeak," he said. "I think the dog must have caught him. I wonder if it did." He wiped his eyes and tried not to cry. "Do you think the dog ate Squeak, Father?"

"I don't think so," Jib said. "A mouse can run very fast."

"But where can he be?"

"He must have run back to the deep woods where he used to live," Jib said. "He'll be all right there."

"But I won't see him again," Nipper said. "Do you think I'll see him again?"

"No," Jib said. "I don't suppose so."

It was getting dark when they got back to Tiddletown. The air was cold, and smoke was coming from the chimneys of the little houses. When Jib and Nipper got to their house, Brindle and Trinket were in the front yard. Jib gave Brindle the fish.

"What fine fat minnows," she said. "What a grand dinner we'll be having tonight." Then she looked again at Jib and Nipper and stopped smiling. "What's the matter?" she said.

So Jib and Nipper began to tell all about the STOMPERS. They told about the two huge STOMPERS and the little one with the big black dog. Jib let Nipper tell how Squeak had saved the day. Nipper told all about it, and then he began to cry.

"Don't cry, Nipper," Trinket said. "Come here."

She took Nipper's hand and pulled him to the front door of the cottage. "Look," she said.

A fire was burning in the fireplace. In front of the fire was a big brown lump. It was Squeak.

"He's been into my things again," Trinket said. "I was about to throw him out. But now I guess I'll let him stay."

Jib came into the house. "Yes," he said. "Let Squeak stay. He saved the day."

2. Trinket's Silver Cup

It had not been a good day for Trinket Tooley. In fact, it had started out to be nothing but trouble.

There had been berry muffins for breakfast. The muffins weren't the bad part. Berry muffins were one of Trinket's favorite things. The bad part was that Trinket got only two.

When Trinket's mother made berry muffins, she always made a dozen. Three for herself, Brindle. And three for Jib, Trinket's father. And three for Nipper, who was Trinket's little brother. And, of course, the other three were Trinket's. But this morning when she was ready for her last muffin— it wasn't there. Nobody knew where it had gone. Nipper said he hadn't taken it. So did Brindle and Jib.

Trinket looked at the empty dish and at the table all around it. There was nothing there. Then she looked down at the floor. Something was sticking out from under the tablecloth. It wasn't a muffin. It was long and thin and gray. It looked like a mouse's tail. Trinket grabbed it and pulled, and out came a fat brown lump. It was Squeak, Nipper's pet mouse, and there were crumbs on his whiskers.

"Your awful mouse ate my muffin," Trinket said to her brother.

"I didn't see him eat it," Nipper said. "What makes you think he ate it?"

"Look at his whiskers," Trinket said.

Squeak put out his long pink tongue and licked.

"I don't see anything but whiskers," Nipper said.

Trinket jumped up. "He took it when we weren't looking. He's a sneak. His name isn't Squeak—it's Sneak. Sneak! Sneak! Sneak!"

She ran out the back door and slammed it behind her. Then she sat down on the back steps. She put her chin in her hands and frowned at the ground. She frowned at a beetle that happened to be passing. She even frowned at the blue sky and sunshine.

The back door opened, and Trinket's father came out. "Oh, there you are," he said, smiling.

Trinket went on frowning.

Jib held out a basket full of seeds. "You might as well feed the quarks," he said, "since you've finished your breakfast."

Trinket frowned harder. "I don't want to feed the quarks," she said. "I hate to feed the quarks. I hate quarks."

Jib stopped smiling. "We all HAVE to do things we hate now and then. I'd really hate to punish somebody—but I might HAVE to."

Trinket took the basket and stomped down the path. "I hate quarks," she said to the blue sky and the sunshine. She stomped all the way to the quark house. In the pen by the quark house, the quarks were squawking and pecking. They pecked in the feed pans and they pecked on the ground and they pecked each other. When they weren't pecking, they ran in circles and fell over their own feet. Quarks always fell over their own feet.

"Ugh!" Trinket said. "Quarks!"

People said that in the olden days quarks were called chickens. Only they were much bigger then. The STOMPERS kept chickens for eggs and feathers and chicken dinners. Chickens were very useful—for the STOMPERS. So the Tiddlers had tried to keep chickens too.

But chickens were too big for Tiddlers. They were too big to feed and too big to catch and much too big to cook. So the Tiddlers, who had had more magic in those days, magicked the chickens to make them smaller. After that, they called them quarks.

Trinket looked through the fence. The quarks were still scratching and pecking and falling down. The trouble with quarks, Trinket thought, was that the magic hadn't worked too well. Some parts of the quarks were smaller than others. Their feet weren't small enough. And their brains were a lot too small. "Quarks!" Trinket said again. "Ugh!"

Feeding the quarks was just the way it always was. A big mess. The quarks ran in circles and stepped on everything. They stepped in the feeding pans and tipped them over. They stepped on each other. One of them stepped in a nest and broke some eggs. The egg goo got on its big feet. Then it stepped on Trinket's new shoes.

After the quarks were fed, things didn't get any better. The next bad thing happened when Trinket went to see her best friend, Dimity Daw. The bad thing was that nobody was home. Trinket couldn't believe it. There were just too many Daws to go away all at once. Somebody was always home at the Daws' house. Always. But not today.

Trinket waited for a while, but no one came. Then she started to walk home. On the way she ran into more trouble. Two of them. Twin troubles!

The Tattle twins lived next door to the Tooleys. Their names were Dollop Tattle and Duffle Tattle, but their middle names were Trouble. Dollop Trouble Tattle and Duffle Trouble Tattle had haystack hair and pebble eyes. They yelled instead of talking. Their smiles looked like jack-o'-lanterns.

Trinket was halfway home when she heard a noise behind her. She turned around quickly. Dollop jumped out from one side of a bush and Duffle from the other. Or else it was the other way around. No one could tell them apart. Dollop threw a berry at Trinket, and Duffle threw a radish. Or else it was the other way around. They yelled at her and called her names. Then they ran away laughing.

That was too much. Trinket couldn't take any more. She couldn't take any more sneaky mice or dumb quarks or twin Troubles. She turned off the path, pushed between some bushes, and climbed over a fence. Then she started off into the forest. And that was when everything started to change.

It was cool in the forest. The light was soft and green. Far away a bird was singing a lonely song. After a while, Trinket stopped frowning. She picked a violet and put it in her yellow hair. Before long she began to sing too. Her song was lonely like the bird's, but singing it made her feel better. Sometimes it was good to be alone and a little bit sad. It was much better than being angry. She walked along through the violets, singing the lonely song. Then she looked down, and there it was. The silver cup.

At first, all she saw was a shining silver sliver. Most of the cup was covered with earth. But the earth was soft. It didn't take long to uncover the whole cup. It was beautiful. As beautiful as bird songs and violets.

Trinket brushed the dirt off the cup. Then she held it up to the sunlight. Silver vines went around and around the cup. On the vines were flowers of silver and gold. The sunlight danced on the shining flowers. Trinket put the cup down in the grass. Then she sat down beside it and looked at it for a long time. At last, she picked it up and went home.

The next day Trinket was reading in her room when the door opened. It was Nipper.

"Hello," he said.

"Hello," Trinket said. "Did you want something?"

"Have you seen my—" Nipper said, and then he stopped. He was staring at the windowsill where the silver cup was sitting. "What's that?" he asked.

"I'm not sure," Trinket said. "It looks like a cup. But it's too big for a Tiddler teacup, and it's too little for a STOMPER one. But it is very beautiful, isn't it? I found it in the forest."

Nipper ran to the window and picked up the cup. He turned it around and around in his hands. Then he turned it upside down and put it on his head. He looked in Trinket's mirror. "I like it," he said.

"Put it down," Trinket said.

Nipper put the cup down on the table. Then he went out of the room, walking backward. All the way out he looked at the cup and whacked the air with both hands. "Whack!" he said. "Jab! Poke! I got you, Dollop. Take that, Duffle."

"What ARE you doing?" Trinket said, but Nipper didn't answer. When he had gone, Trinket picked up the cup and put it back on the window-sill. She went on reading. Now and then she looked at the silver cup in the sunny window.

A little later the door opened again, and Brindle came in with the dust mop. She had dusted half-way across the room when she saw the cup.

"What's that?" she said. "Where did you get it? How long have you had it? Why didn't you tell me about it?"

"Which answer do you want first?" Trinket said.

So her mother asked all the questions over again, one at a time. Trinket answered them all. Then Brindle picked up the cup and said, "Let's show it to your father."

Jib was mending a chair in the kitchen. Nipper was sitting on the floor playing with Squeak. When Jib saw the cup, he put down his tools and picked it up. He asked the same questions Brindle had asked. When Trinket had answered all the questions again, Jib put the cup in the middle of the kitchen table. All the Tooleys stood around the table and looked at it.

"It's an odd thing," Jib said. "It's too small to be

a STOMPER teacup. Perhaps it was made for a STOMPER baby. But that makes it just the right size for Tiddler folk. It could be very useful."

"I found it," Trinket said in a small voice.

"Yes, of course," Jib said. "But you must not be selfish. You know that we Tiddlers need things made of metal. This cup would be just right for carrying quark food. You know how the quark seed always falls through the basket. This cup would be much better."

"Oh, no," Brindle said. "It's too nice for quark food. I think it should be used as a porridge pot. You know how much I need a new porridge pot."

"But I need it," Nipper said. "Every day I get into pole fights with Dollop and Duffle, and every day they whack me on the head. The whacks wouldn't hurt if I had a silver helmet. If I had it, I could win all the pole fights."

Trinket stomped her foot. "But it's mine," she said. "I found it."

They all looked at her.

"You could use it when you feed the quarks," Jib said.

"You could help me make the porridge in it," Brindle said.

"You could watch me beat up the Tattle twins," Nipper said.

"No," Trinket said. "That's not what it's for. It's mine, and I don't want to do any of those things with it."

"What DO you want to do with it?" Jib asked.

"I . . . I just want to look at it," Trinket said. "I just want it to be something beautiful that is all mine."

"Well," Jib said, "I think you are being selfish." He sat down on a kitchen chair and started to light his pipe. "Tooleys are not selfish people. Perhaps Trinket should go to her room and think about being a good Tooley. Don't you think so, Mother?"

"No," Brindle said. "I don't think that would help. I think we must just talk to Trinket. We must help her to understand how bad it is to be selfish. We must talk to her about how Tooleys are never selfish. We must help her to want to be a good Tooley. Don't you think so?"

"I don't think so," Nipper said. "I think we should whack her on the head."

"I don't want to go to my room," Trinket said. "And I don't want a talking-to. And if you whack me on the head, Nipper, I'll whack you back." But no one heard what she was saying. Jib and Brindle were talking in loud voices about quark pans and porridge pots. And Nipper was jumping around whacking the air with both hands.

"Whack! Jab! Poke!" Nipper was saying. He jumped around the room, past Jib and Brindle and past Trinket. He jumped past the windows and the door. "Whack!" he said. "Poke! Whack!" Then he stopped and said, "Hello, Mistress Mayor."

Jib and Brindle stopped talking. They both went to the front window. A woman was walking by the house. She was taller than most Tiddlers, and she had lots of white hair piled high on her head. On top of all the hair was a tiny hat with a big pink feather. The feather hung down over her right eye. She was carrying a big walking stick.

"It's Mistress Muggins," Jib said. He took Brindle's arm and tried to pull her back from the window. "Look out," he said. "She'll see you."

Mistress Muggins was the mayor of the village. She had been mayor of the village for a long time. Some people in Tiddletown thought someone else might be a better mayor. Jib thought so too. Jib thought he would be a much better mayor. But

Mistress Muggins had been mayor for so long no one could even remember how it happened. And most people thought it was too late to do anything about it.

Brindle looked at Jib's hand on her arm. "Why don't you want Mistress Muggins to see us?" she asked.

"Because she'll want to come in," he said. "And then she'll want to tell us what to do, just because she is the mayor. And there are too many mayors in this house already."

Brindle pulled her arm away from Jib's hand. Then she waved it out the window. "Hello, Mistress Muggins," she called.

Mistress Muggins stopped and put her hand up to her ear. When Brindle called again, the mayor nodded her head three times. She waved her walking stick in the air. Then she marched up the path with her pink feather bouncing and her walking stick thumping the ground. She bounced and thumped into the Tooleys' house and nodded her head three times.

"What can I do for you, my good people?" she asked grandly.

"Nothing, thank you," Jib said.

"Dear Mistress Mayor," Brindle said. "You could help us decide something. Something about a silver cup."

"A silver cup," the mayor said. "Aha! Tell me about the silver cup."

So the Tooleys told about the silver cup and what they wanted to do with it. Jib told about feeding the quarks. Brindle told about making porridge. Nipper told about pole fights with the Tattle twins. And Trinket told how the cup sat on her windowsill and looked beautiful.

When they were through with the telling, the mayor said, "I see. I see. And now may I see this cup, if you please?"

Trinket ran to her room and came back with the cup. Mistress Muggins put the cup on the mantel over the fireplace. She stepped back and looked at it with her head tilted to the left. Then she stepped back again and tilted her head to the right. At last she thumped the floor three times with her walking stick. "I have decided," she said. "The cup is very beautiful. It is much too beautiful for quarks or porridge or pole whacks. It should be only to look at."

"Hooray," Trinket said. "I win. I win."

Mistress Muggins thumped again with her stick. "AND—" she said, "it is also too beautiful for one person's bedroom. It must stay right here on the mantel." Then the mayor thumped once more with her walking stick, nodded to each of the Tooleys, and marched grandly out of the house.

"Humph!" Jib said, "What did I tell you?"

"Well, I never!" Brindle said.

"I hate Mistress Muggins," Nipper said.

"But it was mine," Trinket said.

They all frowned at each other.

Then, one by one, they all looked at the silver cup. The sunlight came in through the window and shone on the gold and silver flowers. Little specks of gold and silver light danced through the room. They danced over the dark walls and across the dull floor. Some of them danced on the Tooleys' faces and in their eyes.

Nipper moved first. He went up to the mantel and ran his fingers slowly across the shining flowers. Then Jib picked up the cup and moved it to the center of the mantel. Brindle used her apron to wipe a speck of dust off the rim. Trinket took a violet out of her yellow hair and put it in the cup. Then they all looked at each other and smiled.

Jib kissed Brindle on the cheek. He patted Trinket on the head and picked Nipper up and hugged him. Then he walked to the door and looked out. All the other Tooleys looked out too. Away down the road, Mistress Muggins was still bouncing and thumping.

"Well, well," Jib said, "what do you know? I guess no one is wrong all of the time. Not even our mayor."

3. Brindle's Visitor

"Listen to that thunder," Jib said.

Nipper pushed back his chair and ran to the window. "Oh, look," he called. "Come see. Come see the lightning. Isn't it grand?"

Jib and Trinket got up from the dinner table and went to the window. "Oooh!" they said. "Oh, look! Look at that one."

"Come see, Mother," Trinket called to Brindle. "Come to the window."

Brindle shivered. "No, thanks," she said. "I hate storms. You know I hate storms."

It was true. The wind roaring and the rain pounding made her shiver, and the crash of thunder made her want to hide her head. She didn't know why she hated storms, but she always had.

Nipper came back to finish his dinner. "I think storms are exciting," he said. "Why do you hate them, Mother?"

"I don't know why," Brindle said. "I wish I did."

"Why do you wish you did?" Nipper asked.

Trinket sighed. "Why do you ask WHY so much?" she said to Nipper. She rolled her eyes way up. "Why do little brothers ask WHY so much?"

"Big sisters ask WHY too," Nipper said. "Big sisters ask little brothers WHY they ask WHY so much."

"That's different," Trinket said.

"WHY is it different?" Nipper asked.

"That's enough about WHY," Brindle said. She smiled at Nipper. "It's all right to ask," she said, "but I'm not sure I can answer. Perhaps I wish I knew why because . . ." She stopped to think for a while. Then she said, "Perhaps if I knew why I hate storms, I wouldn't hate them so much."

"Well, cheer up," Jib said. "I don't think this one can last much longer."

But Jib was wrong. The storm lasted all that night. All night long Brindle shivered and shook. She hid her head under her pillow and tried to sleep. It was almost morning when a loud crash of thunder made her sit straight up in bed. Jib was still sound asleep. The thunder rolled and rolled. At last it died away, but the noises went on. The wind roared and the rain pounded. Things slid across the roof and scratched at the windows. Brindle tried to go back to sleep, but she couldn't. All she could do was hide her head and try not to hear the storm.

But even under the pillow she could hear the wind and the rain. Rain and wind and—something else. Brindle took her head out from under the pillow and listened. Then she sat up again and listened to the new sound.

At first it sounded like Nipper's pet mouse squeaking. And then it sounded like a STOMPER animal. Or more like a baby STOMPER animal. After a while it began to sound like someone crying. Brindle got out of bed and went to the window. The sound was louder there.

It must be, Brindle thought. It must be someone crying. She lit a candle and went downstairs.

It was dark and cold in the kitchen. Brindle stood still and listened. The crying sound went on and on. Then there was a soft, thumping noise. It sounded like someone knocking softly on the kitchen door. Brindle tiptoed across the floor and put her ear close to the door. There it was again, close to her ear. Sob—sob—gasp—gasp. And then, thump! thump! thump!

Brindle took a deep breath. She held the candle up high. Then she unlocked the door and opened it a tiny crack.

Someone—someone very small—was lying on the doorstep in the pouring rain. A little child, Brindle thought, no bigger than Nipper.

"Land-o'-livin'!" she said. "What are you doing out there in the rain? Come in. Come in at once."

But as Brindle bent down to help, the tiny person jumped up. It backed away toward the garden holding out its tiny hands.

"No, no," it said in a high, thin voice, "don't touch me."

Brindle gasped in surprise. By the light of the candle, she could see that the small person was not a child, after all. She was about as tall as Nipper, but she would not weigh nearly as much. As light as an eggshell, Brindle thought. Or maybe a feather. And her face was not the face of a child. It was not a young face or an old one. It was a face that would never get old. "Land-o'-livin'!" Brindle gasped. "You're a fairy!"

"I am Moonbeam," the tiny person said. "And

I'm cold and wet and tired. Would you mind stepping out of the way so I can come in?"

Brindle jumped back. "Of course," she said. "Come in. Come right in."

The fairy came into the room. She was not flying, but she seemed to barely touch the floor with the tips of her tiny toes. Brindle looked for her wings. Fairies were supposed to have wings, but this one didn't seem to have any. Brindle lit a lamp and looked again, and there they were.

She had wings, all right. Two wet and ragged shadows hung down her back like torn bits of raincloud. In her right hand was a small, golden wand with a bend in the middle. She was, indeed, a fairy. A wet and ragged fairy with soggy wings, a bent wand, a red nose, and a bad case of shivers.

"You poor little thing," Brindle said. "You sit right down here in the big chair. I'll have a fire going in a minute."

Soon the fire was burning brightly, and the house was warm and cozy. In the kitchen Brindle was trying to scramble quark eggs and keep one eye on her special visitor. My, my, she kept saying to herself. Won't Jib and the children be surprised? And wait until I tell Fancie Daw. Fancie is always

telling me how she saw a fairy once. But she has never had one in her own house. I'm sure that no one else in Tiddletown has ever had a fairy for a visitor.

A few minutes later, Jib came down the stairs. Right behind him were Trinket and Nipper. And, of course, Squeak was right behind Nipper. Brindle put her finger to her lips. "Shhh!" she said. "Look in the parlor, in front of the fire."

They tiptoed to the door and peeked in.

"Great jumping jack-o'-lanterns!" Jib said. "Would you look at that!"

"I'm looking!" Nipper said. "What is it?"

"Ooooh! She's beautiful," Trinket said. "She's the most beautiful thing I've ever seen."

"She's a fairy," Brindle said, "and her name is Moonbeam."

Moonbeam was still sitting in Jib's big chair by the fire. She was dry now. Her nose wasn't red anymore. She had great green eyes. Her long hair was the color of moonlight. She was beautiful indeed.

"Well, don't stand there staring," she said. "You may come in, but not too near." She looked at Brindle. "And you may bring me something to eat now. And please take the mouse with you. Fairies are not fond of mice."

"Oh, yes," Brindle said. "I will. I'll keep Squeak in the kitchen with me."

So Brindle pulled Squeak into the kitchen and shut the door. While she worked she tiptoed around and over the fat mouse. A few minutes later, she tiptoed into the parlor with toast and jam and eggs. The other Tooleys were sitting on the floor around Moonbeam's chair. Moonbeam took the food and began to eat.

"Oh, dear," she said, wrinkling her tiny nose. "What strange food. Don't you have any proper food like bee bread and green-moon cheese?"

"I'm afraid not," Brindle said.

"This will have to do, then," Moonbeam said. She took a tiny, careful bite and chewed slowly. "Hmmm!" she said. "Hmmm!" She began to eat more quickly.

"Did you hear, Mother?" Trinket said. "While you were in the kitchen, Moonbeam told us what happened to her. She was lost in the storm. The storm wrinkled her wings and bent her wand. With a broken wand, she couldn't fly or find her way. That's why she came to our house."

"Yes, I thought it was something like that," Brindle said.

When Moonbeam's plate was almost empty, she got up and stood in front of the fireplace. She spread out her silvery wings. The wings fluttered slowly up and down and back and forth. The dancing firelight made a golden circle around her lovely head.

"Tell us about your wand," Trinket said in a breathless voice. "Please, Mistress Moonbeam."

"Oh, yes," Nipper said. "Tell what your wand does when it's not broken. Please tell us about that."

"A magic wand," Moonbeam said, "can do wonders. All kinds of wonders."

"Hmmm!" Jib said. He was wondering if a wand could make somebody mayor of the village.

Brindle nodded her head slowly. She was wondering if a wand could make someone stop being afraid of storms.

Trinket twisted some of her yellow hair around her fingers. She wondered if a wand could make somebody a new dress for the May Day fair.

Nipper rubbed the bump on his head where Duffle had whacked him, or else it was Dollop.

He was wondering what was the worst thing a wand could do to twins.

"I could show you magical things," Moonbeam said, "if only . . ." She looked sadly at the bent wand.

Jib held out his hand. "May I see it?" he asked. "Perhaps I can fix it."

"Oh, no!" Moonbeam put the wand behind her back. "Wands are not for human hands."

"But we're not humans," Nipper said. "We're Tiddlers."

Moonbeam laughed. Her laugh sounded like tiny silver bells. "Well," she said, "a little less than human, perhaps. But not at all magical. Fairies, on the other hand, are very magical."

Brindle put her hands on her hips. She tipped her head to one side and looked carefully at her visitor. Somehow, the golden circle around Moonbeam's head didn't seem as bright. Humph! Brindle thought. Less than human, indeed. But the rest of the Tooleys were still staring at the fairy with their eyes full of moonbeams.

"Tiddlers can do magic," Brindle said. "We can blur the eyes of the STOMPERS. That's magic, isn't it?"

Moonbeam laughed again. "Well, I suppose that might seem like magic to some people." She smiled at Nipper. "The wand will mend itself, but it will take time. Perhaps I can show you some magic tomorrow."

Then Moonbeam looked at the warm fire. She turned and looked at Jib's big cozy chair. Next, she looked at the almost empty plate. She picked up the last piece of toast and jam and ate it slowly. "Or maybe next week," she said. "Perhaps the wand will mend itself by next week."

So Moonbeam stayed all that day and the next and the next, and the Tooleys learned a great many things about their visitor.

They learned that fairies don't have real houses. They don't because they can live in wonderful places. Places like floating lily pads or magic toadstools.

"Sounds cold to me," Nipper said.

Moonbeam laughed. "Not at all." She cuddled up in Jib's big chair and held out her hands to the fire. "We keep warm and dry by magic," she said. "We don't have to clean and dust and make fires."

"That sounds lovely," Trinket said. "But how do you cook dinner?"

"We don't bother with cooking," Moonbeam said. She picked up one of Brindle's special tea cakes and nibbled thoughtfully. "We eat wonderful magic things like bee bread and honeydew and green-moon cheese. Magic food is much better than ordinary food." Moonbeam smiled sweetly at Brindle. "Is there another tea cake?" she asked.

"I could make some more," Brindle said.

"Oh, lovely," Moonbeam said. "And with much more raspberry jam this time, if you please."

On the third or fourth day, Brindle asked if she could bring a neighbor to meet Moonbeam. "Fancie Daw lives next door," she told Moonbeam. "She's always going on about fairies. I'm sure she'd love to meet you."

"Oh, no," Moonbeam said. "I couldn't. Fairies are quiet, secret people. We need to be alone."

"Well, then," Brindle said, "I'm sure you are tired of having so many Tooleys around. We'd best be getting on with our work, anyway. Come on, everyone. Moonbeam needs to be quiet and secret."

"Oh, no," Moonbeam said. "I was just telling Trinket and Nipper about the time I turned a gray wolf into a butterfly. And I want Jib to hear too.

But you can go now, Brindle, if you need to make dinner. Tea cakes, perhaps. Yes! I think we'd like tea cakes and jam."

As the days went by, there were other things that Brindle learned about her visitor. She learned that fairies can't sleep in beds because they might wrinkle their wings. At night Moonbeam stayed right where she was in Jib's big chair, so the fire had to burn all night long. And since everyone else was busy listening, Brindle learned a lot about finding firewood.

Another thing Brindle learned was the kinds of things fairies like best to eat, such as tea cakes and raspberry jam. And the kinds of things they won't eat, such as quark soup. So when Brindle made soup for the Tooleys, she also had to make tea cakes and jam for Moonbeam.

So Brindle learned how to make two dinners at once. And since Squeak had to stay in the kitchen, she also learned how to make two dinners at once without tripping over a fat mouse. As the days passed, Brindle learned a lot about having a fairy for a visitor.

There was one thing, however, that Brindle could not learn, no matter how hard she tried. She couldn't learn when Moonbeam was planning to go home to her lily pads and magic toadstools. Whenever Brindle tried to find out, Moonbeam would sigh and look sadly at her wand.

"I don't know," she would say. "I would like to go soon, but I just don't know. My poor wand is still broken."

Brindle looked carefully at the wand many times. The bend was all gone. Brindle thought it looked just fine. But when she said so, someone always told her that she didn't understand about such things. Sometimes it was Moonbeam who told her, and sometimes it was Trinket or Nipper. Once in a while, it was even Jib.

"What do we Tiddler folk know about wands?" Jib said, smiling at Moonbeam.

"Humph! We 'less than human' folk, you mean?" Brindle said softly.

"What's that?" Jib asked.

"Nothing," Brindle said. "Nothing at all."

It was a week later, or maybe almost two, that Brindle came down to the kitchen early. Jib and the children were still asleep upstairs. As she came quietly down the stairs, she began to hear a sound.

It was a soft airy sound like small puffs of wind. It was coming from the parlor.

Brindle tiptoed to the parlor door and peeked in. The small noise was the sound of Moonbeam's wings as she flew slowly around and around the room. The moment she saw Brindle, she came lightly down to the floor. She climbed into Jib's big chair.

"How nice that you can fly again," Brindle said.

"Oh, not well," Moonbeam said. "Not really well. I feel sure I would not be able to fly very far."

"I see," Brindle said. "It's a funny thing about feelings. I feel sure that I will not be able to make tea cakes this morning."

"But I like tea cakes for breakfast," Moonbeam said.

"Then why don't you make them?" Brindle said. "Now that your wand is working, you could make them with magic, couldn't you?"

Moonbeam laughed like silver bells. "Oh, dear," she said. "You just don't understand about wands. Wands make only magic food such as bee bread and green-moon cheese. Wands do only magic. You seem to think that wands do ordinary things such as making tea cakes. Or cleaning houses. Or making fires. Or opening doors. Well, you are quite wrong. You don't know a thing about—"

"Wait a minute," Brindle said. "You mean wands don't do any of those things?"

"Of course not," Moonbeam said.

"They don't open doors?"

"Of course not," Moonbeam said.

"I see," Brindle said. "I see." She walked toward Jib's chair.

"Don't touch me," Moonbeam said.

"Why not?" Brindle asked.

"Because fairies may not be touched by human hands."

"Don't worry," Brindle said. "My hands are less than human."

Brindle picked Moonbeam up very gently and carried her into the kitchen. She opened the back door and put the fairy down on the top step. She closed the door and latched it. Then she went back into the kitchen and started breakfast. She did not make tea cakes.

While Brindle was making breakfast, she worried about how Jib and Trinket and Nipper would feel when they saw that Moonbeam was gone. She wondered how they would feel and what they would say.

"Where's Moonbeam?" was what they said. Jib said it first, and then Trinket and Nipper. "Where did Moonbeam go?"

"I don't know," Brindle said. "At least, I'm not certain. But I feel quite sure she's gone back to her lily pad. Or perhaps to her toadstool." She looked from one face to another with a worried frown.

Nipper smiled. "Now can Squeak and I play in the parlor again?" he said.

"And can we do something besides listening?" Trinket said with a giggle.

"And can I have my big chair back?" Jib said.

Brindle laughed. "Yes, of course you can," she said.

"And somebody I know can stop making so many tea cakes," Jib said. And all the Tooleys laughed.

After that winter Brindle didn't mind storms quite as much.

"Aren't you afraid of storms anymore, Mother?" Nipper asked when Brindle went to the window to watch the lightning.

"Not as much," Brindle said. "Maybe it's because I've learned something."

"What, Mother?" Nipper said. "What did you learn?"

"Well," Brindle said, "I guess I've learned that there's no use worrying about lightning. Because there's nothing you can do about it. And there's no use worrying about what might blow in. Because there IS something you can do about THAT."

Nipper looked puzzled. "What can you do about what blows in?" he asked. "What can you do, Mother?"

Brindle smiled a secret smile. "You can pick it up and put it on the doorstep," she said.

4. Nipper's Little Stomper

It was a warm afternoon in late summer. Brindle and Jib had gone to the market. Nipper had gone off somewhere or other. Trinket was home alone.

It was too hot in the cottage, so Trinket went outside to read. She made herself a secret place in some tall grass. She bent the grass down to make a round room with cool green walls. When the room was finished, she sat down and opened her book. She had only read one page when she heard somebody whispering. Then she heard somebody else whispering. The second somebody sounded like Nipper.

"Oh-oh," Trinket said. A whispering little brother is usually a bad sign. She stood up carefully and quietly and peeked out over the top of the grass. She peeked out just in time to see Nipper and his best friend, Tuck Barley, tiptoeing into the house. Nipper was leading the way. He put his finger up to his lips. Then he opened the door and held it for Tuck. Tuck was carrying a great big sack.

"Oh-oh," Trinket said again. "I wonder." She was wondering what she ought to do. On the one hand, it was nice in her secret spot, and she was reading a good book. I'd much rather stay right here, she told herself. But on the other hand, Nipper and Tuck—and a great big sack—and whispering—could add up to only one thing—TROUBLE. I'd better go see what they're doing, and tell them to stop, she decided.

Trinket was just about to leave her secret spot when the back door opened again. Nipper and Tuck came out. This time they were both carrying the sack. It looked a lot bigger. They tiptoed down the steps, across the backyard, and started off on the path to the woods.

"Hmmm!" Trinket said. She waited until the boys were almost out of sight, and then she went after them. She ran across the backyard and down the path. She ran on tiptoe, being careful not to get too close. She didn't want the boys to see her. She just wanted to follow them and see what they were up to.

It was cooler in the woods. The light was dim

and greenish. Trinket could get closer without being seen. Now and then she got close enough to hear what the boys were saying. She was running from one hiding place to another when she heard Nipper say, "Stop! I have to rest for a minute. That sack is too heavy."

Trinket sat down behind a bush and listened.

"I'm tired too," Tuck said. "Let's sit down and rest."

"All right," Nipper said, "but not for long. We have to hurry. It must be awful hungry."

"Yes," Tuck said. "And it might get away. If it wakes up before we get back, it might get out of the hut. It might run away."

Oh, dear, Trinket thought, they've got another STOMPER animal. Nip and Tuck were always trying to make pets of STOMPER animals, and it simply didn't work. Squeak, the mouse, came the closest to working, and that wasn't very close.

Before Squeak, there had been a rabbit who ate half the garden, a lamb who ate half the roof, and a kitten who ate three quarks and took a small bite out of Nipper.

What on earth do they have this time? Trinket wondered.

A few minutes later, the boys got up. They picked up their sack and started off. Trinket followed close behind.

Before long, they came to a small clearing in the middle of the deep woods. At the edge of the clearing was a huge wooden building. Long ago a STOMPER woodsman had built it to rest in when he was out in the deep forest. To the woodsman it would have been only a tiny hut, but to Trinket it looked huge indeed.

Nipper and Tuck hurried to the hut. They put down their sack and began to pull at the door. They both had to pull with all their might to open it a tiny crack. Then they tiptoed inside.

Trinket ran to the door and peeked through the crack. At first the hut seemed to be empty, except for Nipper and Tuck. But then Trinket noticed an old iron stove in one corner. In another corner there was a pile of dry grass. Nipper and Tuck were looking toward the grass pile. Trinket looked again—and couldn't believe her eyes. Something was asleep on the grass in the corner of the hut. It wasn't a rabbit or a lamb or a kitten. It was a baby. The biggest baby that Trinket had ever seen.

"Oh!" Trinket said. "Oh, dear! Oh, dear!"

Nipper and Tuck turned around. "Trinket!" Nipper whispered. "You followed us, you dirty rat! Are you going to tell?" Then he squeezed back out through the crack and grabbed her arm. "Please don't tell, Trinket," he begged. "It's ours. We're going to keep it."

"You can't," Trinket said. "You can't keep it. It's a baby. It belongs to somebody. It belongs to a STOMPER mother and father."

Nipper stuck out his chin. "I don't care. I don't care if it belongs to them or not. They must not have liked it much, or they wouldn't have lost it."

Tuck was still in the hut, but his head was sticking out through the crack. "Finders keepers," he said.

Just then, another voice said something. A voice from inside the hut. What it said was "MAMA!"

Trinket and Nipper squeezed back inside.

The baby was sitting up on the pile of grass. It had huge blue eyes, a round pink face and lots of curly brown hair. Its arms and hands were pink and fat. It was wearing a light blue playsuit. Its face was dirty except where tears had made little clean rivers down its cheeks. "Mama?" it said again. It was looking at Trinket. "Where Mama?" it asked her.

Trinket shook her head. "I don't know," she said. "I don't know where your mama is."

The baby made a sad noise, and big tears spilled out of its huge blue eyes. "Maaa-maaa," it said.

Trinket took a step forward. "Oh, the poor little thing," she said.

"Look out!" Nipper said. "It hugs! It hugged Tuck so hard he couldn't breathe for five minutes!"

Trinket stopped. The baby rubbed its eyes with both fists and began to cry. "Poor little thing," Trinket said. Then she looked at Tuck and Nipper. "Can it walk?" she asked.

"Of course it can walk," Tuck said. "How do you think it got here? We sure didn't carry it. It must weigh twice as much as Mistress Muggins."

"And it talks a little," Trinket said. "It's not a really new baby." She took a step closer. "Listen, little STOMPER," she said to the baby. "What's your name?"

The little STOMPER stopped crying and looked at her. It sniffed and gasped a few times. "Name?" it said in a teary voice. It nodded its head and

pointed to the middle of its forehead. Then it said something that sounded like "Nelly."

"Nelly," Trinket said. "Its name is Nelly."

"What kind of a name is that?" Nipper asked. "Is that a boy's name or a girl's name?"

"I don't know," Trinket said.

"I think it said *Smelly,*" Tuck said. "I think its name is *Smelly.*"

Trinket sniffed. She could see what Tuck meant. The baby didn't smell too good.

Tuck and Nipper looked at each other and giggled.

"Stop that," Trinket said. "It can't help it. It's only a baby. Or almost." She looked at the little STOMPER. "How old are you, Nelly?" she asked. "Do you know how old you are?"

"Old?" the little STOMPER said. Then it nodded its head and smiled. It was the first time they had seen it smile. It held out one hand. It tipped its head to one side and thought. It put up two fingers. Then it shook its head and took down one finger. It held out one finger and smiled and nodded. "Two," it said.

"See!" Trinket said. "It's two. Or else one."

"Hey," Nipper said, "let's feed it. We've been forgetting to feed it."

"Yes," Tuck said. "Let's."

Nipper and Tuck opened the big sack. Nipper took out a loaf of bread. He held it out toward the baby. The baby looked at the bread. "Cookie," it said. "Cookie. Cookie."

"Give it the bread," Tuck said.

Nipper started toward the baby, but then he stopped and backed up. "I'm scared to," he said. "I'm afraid it'll hug me."

"Well, I'll feed it," Trinket said. "Poor little thing. It's starving."

She took the bread to the baby. It didn't hug Trinket. It was too busy eating. It ate the loaf of bread in three bites. Then it ate two more loaves of bread. Then it ate six tea cakes, seven sandwiches, four muffins, five rounds of cheese, and an apple pie. Then it looked around and said, "More."

"Wow-ee!" Nipper said. "It sure eats a lot. I thought we had enough in there for three or four days."

"Where did you get all that food?" Trinket asked. "Besides the things you got at our house?

You got the tea cakes and the cheese at our house, but where did the rest come from?"

"We got some from our kitchen," Tuck said.

"Our mother is going to be angry," Trinket said.

"So is mine," Tuck said.

The baby clapped its hands and said, "More!"

"See?" Trinket said. "You can't keep it. It eats too much."

"I can. I can too." Nipper looked as if he were going to cry. "I want it."

Trinket looked at her little brother. She shook her head. Nipper was so stubborn. "You really can't keep it, Nipper," she said softly. "It would starve. And besides—just look at it. It's dirty. It needs a bath. And it needs its pants changed. How are you going to do that?"

Nipper and Tuck looked at each other. Tuck grinned. "Smelly," he said.

Finally Nipper sighed. "All right," he said. "I guess you're right. We can't keep it. But what are we going to do with it? We can't just leave it here."

"No, of course not," Trinket said. "We've got to take it back where it belongs."

Nipper and Tuck stared at her.

"Back to where the STOMPERS live?" Tuck sounded very surprised. "You know we aren't supposed to go near STOMPER places."

Trinket nodded thoughtfully. Tuck was right, of course. It would be wrong and dangerous. One of the first things the Tiddlers teach their children is to stay as far away from STOMPERS as possible. Trinket herself had never been close to where STOMPERS lived. But she happened to know that some people—some people she knew very well—had broken that rule at least once.

"Well," she said. "I seem to remember that some boys I know went near a STOMPER farm once. I'm not mentioning any names, but I seem to remember those boys bragging about it. Do you remember anything like that, Nipper? Do you and Tuck remember that?"

Tuck and Nipper hung their heads. "Well," Nipper said, "we did get pretty close to a STOMPER farm once."

"All right," Trinket said, "then you can find it again. We'll take Nelly to that farm."

"But how do we know that's where it came from?" Tuck said. "We didn't find it there. We found it way out in the woods."

"It doesn't matter," Trinket said. "All the STOMPERS who live near the deep woods must know each other. The ones at that farm will know who's lost a baby. They'll take it back to its mother and father."

"Hey," Nipper said. "You're right. They probably would." He grabbed the edge of the heavy door. "Come on, Trinket. Help get this door open."

When the door was open, Trinket called to the baby, "Come on, Nelly. Get up. We're going for a walk. We're going home."

"Home," the baby said. "Home, home, home."

First it got up on its hands and feet, and then it stood right up. Trinket gasped. It looked like a baby, all right—fat and round and a little wobbly. But it also looked E-NOR-MOUS!

"Watch out," Nipper said. "Don't get too close to it. It falls down a lot."

They started out through the woods toward the place where Tuck and Nipper had seen the STOMPER farm. It was a long way. The little STOMPER walked slowly. Sometimes it said, "Mama" and "home," and sometimes it cried a little. Every now and then, it tipped over and fell down. It didn't get hurt when it fell down, but after a while it was hard to make it get up again. The sixth or seventh time it fell down, it just sat there and made sad noises.

"It's tired," Trinket said. "Poor little thing." She went close to the baby. "Come on, Baby," she begged. "Get up. Please get up. We have to take you home."

"Home," the baby said. Great fat tears rolled down its cheeks. It rubbed its eyes with both of its fat pink hands.

"Poor Baby," Trinket said. She went closer and patted its leg.

The little STOMPER looked at Trinket. Then it reached out and grabbed her. It grabbed her around the middle and lifted her up off the ground in both of its fat pink hands.

"Look out!" Nipper yelled. "It's got Trinket!"

"It's got her!" Tuck screamed. "Look out! It's going to hug her!"

The baby held Trinket up right in front of its face.

"Put me down, Baby!" Trinket said. "Don't hug me! I might break if you hug me! DON'T!"

The little STOMPER looked at Trinket. "Not break," it said. Then it held Trinket closer.

"It's going to eat her!" Tuck screamed.

"Stop it! Stop it!" Nipper yelled. "Don't eat my sister!"

The little STOMPER kissed Trinket. It kissed her right on the face. Then it put her down carefully on the ground.

Trinket smiled at the little STOMPER. "That's a good baby," she said. "Come on. Let's get up now. We have to get you home."

"Home," the baby said. It got up on its feet, and they started on toward the STOMPER farm.

Not long afterward they came to the edge of the woods. Nipper, who was ahead, stopped suddenly. "Shhh!" he said. "There it is."

In front of them was a huge field with a fence around it. Beyond the field was a house. It was the biggest house Trinket had ever seen.

"Look," she said to the baby. "See the house. Go to the house. Go home. Go to Mama."

The little STOMPER looked where Trinket was pointing. "Home. Mama," it said, and started off toward the house. Trinket and Nipper and Tuck went with it as far as the fence and found a place where it could get under. Then they climbed up on the bottom rail of the fence and watched.

They watched the baby as it walked faster and faster and then tried to run. They saw it fall down. They watched it get up and go on. Then a big dog came out from under the house. The big dog started to bark. The door of the house opened, and a huge woman ran out. She ran to the baby and grabbed it up in her arms. She hugged and kissed it, and it kissed her back.

Trinket and Nipper and Tuck looked at each other and grinned. They climbed down off the fence and started for home. It was late, and they were tired. They had a long way to go. But they were very happy. At least, they were happy at first. But after a while Trinket began to worry.

"We did a dangerous thing," she said to Nipper and Tuck. "We did something we've been told not to do. Over and over and over again we've been told not to go near STOMPER places. If they had seen us, it would have been dangerous for all the Tiddlers."

"But they didn't see us," Tuck said. "Nobody saw us."

"And what if the baby tells them about us?" Trinket said.

"Don't be silly," Nipper said. "It can't tell about us. It doesn't know enough words."

"But it will know enough words soon," Trinket said. "Before long it will know lots more words. And then it will tell the big STOMPERS that there are Tiddler folk in the deep woods."

Trinket was worried, and now Nipper and Tuck were looking worried too.

"It might," Tuck said.

But then Nipper grinned. "It doesn't matter," he said. "Don't you remember when I told Mother and Father about the purple monster I saw behind the quark shed? Don't you remember what they said?"

"They said you were making things up," Trinket said.

"That's right," Nipper said. "And that's what the big STOMPERS will say when our little STOMPER tells about us. They'll say just what Mother and Father said to me. They'll say, 'Listen, Nelly. There's no such thing as Tiddlers.'"

Trinket stared at Nipper for a moment. Then she

grinned. "You know what?" she said. "I think you're right."

Nipper punched Tuck in the ribs. "You hear that?" he said. "She thinks I'm right. For once, Trinket thinks I'm right."

5. Jib and the Drumbies

Jib Tooley had been a farmer all his life, but he had always dreamed of being a drumbie-man.

A farmer makes his living by raising crops and quarks. To raise crops and quarks you have to live in the same place, year in and year out. A drumbie-man, on the other hand, makes his living by raising drumbies. A drumbie herd needs to roam through the wild woods looking for fine, sweet grass. So a drumbie-man lives wild and free, following his herd. Jib thought he would like the life of a drumbie-man.

Of course there were some bad things about being a drumbie-man. The worst of the bad things were the drumbies themselves. Drumbies look like small, shaggy oxen. Just like quarks, they were once STOMPER-size, but long ago they were made smaller by magic. But using magic is always dangerous. The quarks got big feet and small brains. Drumbies got too much WILL power. They also got too much WON'T power.

But Jib liked drumbies. Sometimes he said, "All right, drumbies are a little stubborn. But how could we get along without them?" It was true. The Tiddlers needed drumbies for milk and cheese. They also needed them to pull their carts and plow their fields. Sometimes they used them to ride on. Drumbies carry Tiddler folk and pull their carts and plows—when they feel like it. When they don't feel like it—they WON'T.

But still—Jib liked drumbies. He liked to wear drumbie-man boots. He also liked to sing the songs the drumbie-men sang around their campfires at night.

On a high shelf in the parlor Jib kept a lot of books about the olden days. Nearly every night after dinner, he took down a book and sat in his big chair by the fire. The books were about drumbie-men and how they lived in the wild woods in the olden days. In those days drumbie-men had many dangerous and exciting adventures. They had to climb mountains and swim rivers. Sometimes they were chased by wild animals. And sometimes they were almost caught by STOMPERS. Jib read the books over and over.

Brindle thought that Jib's drumbie-man dream

was funny. So did Trinket and Nipper. Sometimes Trinket and Nipper teased their father about being a pretend drumbie-man. Sometimes, when they saw him reading about drumbie-men in the olden days, they would start to sing drumbie-man songs in loud voices. Or else they would run through the house pretending they were riding a galloping drumbie.

But Jib didn't mind. He went on reading his stories, and now and then, he still daydreamed about selling his farm and buying a grand herd of drumbies. And every spring he looked forward to plowing time when he would own a fine team of drumbies—for a short time. Of course, the drumbies really belonged to Bluster Swag, but every year Jib rented them to do his spring plowing.

Bluster Swag was the only real drumbie-man in Tiddletown. In the winter Bluster lived in the village with his wife, Phobia, and their children, Petal and Jingo. But the rest of the year he was off in the wild woods with his herdsmen and most of his fine drumbies. While he was gone Phobia milked the milking drumbies, and Jingo rented the plowing drumbies. And Bluster Swag rode wild and free. Jib thought that Bluster Swag led a fine life.

One day in early spring Jib crossed off another number on the calendar on the kitchen wall. He smiled to himself. Then he said to Brindle. "Would you look at that, my dear? Here it is almost plowing time already. What a surprise!"

Brindle smiled. She knew that plowing time would never take Jib by surprise. She knew that he had been crossing off the days for weeks and weeks. But all she said was, "Is it really, my dear? How time flies!"

Right after breakfast Jib went out to check his land. He dug a little here and a little there to see if the earth was ready for plowing. It was. "Glory be!" Jib said. He went back to the house and put on his drumbie-man boots. Then he set off for Bluster Swag's place at the end of the village.

As Jib walked along the dusty road he wondered if Bluster would still be at home. It was almost time for him to set off into the wild woods. Jib hoped he would be there. He liked to talk to Old Bluster. He liked to watch the herdsmen as they got ready for the long summer in the wild woods.

Jib was in luck. When he got to the Swags' place

Bluster was still there. So were the other herdsmen. They were stomping around the yard in their big boots getting ready for the drumbie drive.

"How-de-do," they said when they saw Jib. Drumbie-men always said How-de-do instead of Hello.

"How-de-do," Jib said to Bluster and the other drumbie-men. "Looks to me as how you're almost ready for the long ride." That was the way drumbie-men always talked in the storybooks.

"That's right"—Bluster was grinning— "and it looks to me as how you're ready to start your spring plowing. Go right on into the barn. Jingo will pick you out a fine team."

In the barn a skinny boy with bowlegs was throwing hay down from the loft. The boy was Jingo Swag, and the bowlegs came from riding fat drumbies. You could always tell a drumbie-man by his bowlegs.

When Jib was a boy he thought it would be grand to have bowlegs like a drumbie-man. He had tried to walk bowlegged, but his legs wouldn't bow. He even tried sitting on a fat barrel. Sitting on a barrel was supposed to give you bowlegs. But all Jib got was splinters.

"How-de-do," Jingo said. "You want a team?"

"That's right," Jib said.

Jingo climbed down from the loft. He pointed to the first two drumbies. "How about Brownie and Champ?" he said.

"No, I don't think so," Jib said. "I'll just look around and pick out the ones I want."

Jib walked up and down the barn three times. Then he picked out two fine drumbies. One was light brown and had a white spot on its forehead. "What's its name?" Jib asked.

"Star," Jingo said.

Jib looked at the drumbie. "Why Star?" he asked.

Jingo pointed to the spot on its forehead. "Looks like a star," he said.

Then Jib picked out a big reddish drumbie with white feet. "I'll take that one," he said.

Jingo grinned. "You sure?" he said.

"Of course, I'm sure." Jib said. "Fine-looking animal."

"Drat-you," Jingo said.

Jib frowned at Jingo. "Drat WHO?" he said.

Jingo pointed at the reddish drumbie. "Drat-you! That's his name."

"Oh," Jib said. He didn't ask why the big drumbie was named Drat-you. Maybe he should have, but he didn't.

"Need a plow?" Jingo asked.

"Nope," Jib said. In the storybooks drumbie-men always said Nope. "Got my own plow. I'll take a saddle, though. Think I'd like to ride home."

Then Jib went out to talk to Bluster. When he came back the drumbies were ready to go. There was a saddle on the one named Star. Jib climbed into the saddle. Jingo handed him Drat-you's lead rope.

"Git-up, Drat-you!" Jingo yelled.

They started off down the road.

The ride went well. When Jib and his two fine drumbies got home, Brindle was in the front yard.

"Well," she said, "how did it go? Any trouble?"

"Not a bit," Jib said. "I picked out a fine team."

He put the drumbies in the shed and fed them lots of grass and grain. He cleaned and brushed them and polished their long horns. He sharpened his plow and mended his harness. He spent the whole afternoon in the shed with the drumbies. While he worked he sang drumbie-men songs

such as, "Home in the Wild Wood" and "Git Along, Little Drumbie."

It was almost dark when Jib patted the drumbies' heads for the last time. He sang one last drumbie-man song. Then he told the drumbies to get a good night's rest. The drumbies didn't say anything.

The next morning Jib got up early. He ate his breakfast quickly. Then he hurried out to the shed. He harnessed the drumbies to the plow. He put the reins around his shoulders. He tipped the plow to one side so that it wouldn't dig into the ground until he got to the field. When he called "Git-up!" the drumbies looked at each other. Next they looked back at the plow. Then they started off at a slow walk.

Jib grinned. "No trouble," he said. "I picked out a fine team."

When he got to the field Jib called "Whoa, Star. Whoa, Drat-you." The drumbies stopped. Jib straightened the plow. He dug its sharp blade into the ground. Then he shook the reins. "Git-up!" he said.

The drumbies looked at each other. Next they looked back at the plow. Drat-you shook his head.

Then he said something. He said it in Drumbie language. It sounded like "M-M-M-M-rumph." In drumbie language "M-M-M-M-rumph" means something like "fat chance."

Jib tried being nice. He patted the drumbies. He fed them some grain. He sang to them. He asked them nicely to "git-up." He asked them nicely about fifty times.

While Jib was being nice, nothing much happened. Once or twice Star took two steps forward and three steps back. Drat-you nibbled some grass. He swished his tail. Once he lifted one foot —and used it to scratch behind his ear.

Then Jib tried being not so nice. He yelled. He shook his fists. At last he picked a big switch and gave Drat-you one whack on the back.

When Jib yelled, Drat-you twitched his ears. When Jib shook his fists, Drat-you closed his eyes. But when Jib whacked Drat-you, he put his head down and shook his big horns. Then he ate Jib's switch.

At noon Jib tied the drumbies to a tree at the edge of the field. He went back to the house for his lunch. Nipper and Trinket were away at school. Brindle was at the kitchen stove stirring the soup.

"How did the plowing go?" she asked when Jib came in.

"Don't ask," Jib said.

Brindle turned around. Jib looked stormy. His face was a dark cloud. His eyes were lightning. His voice was thunder.

"I won't," she said.

"You won't what?" Jib rumbled.

"Ask," Brindle said.

After lunch Jib went back to the field. He had decided to try one more time. He untied the drumbies and hitched them to the plow. He took a deep breath. Then he said, "git-up."

Drat-you said, "M-M-M-M-rumph."

Jib said "git-up" nicely about forty-three times. Then he yelled it more than thirty-two times. Then he screamed it at least seventeen times. Finally he jumped up and down and pulled his hair with both hands.

Star and Drat-you turned their big shaggy heads. They watched Jib pull his own hair. They blinked their big, soft drumbie eyes. Then they began to pull.

Jib ran after them and grabbed the plow. They plowed the whole field without stopping. Jib was very happy.

But Jib had three fields. When they got to the second field Drat-you said, "M-M-M-M-rumph" again. Jib thought he knew what to do. Right away he tried jumping up and down and pulling his own hair. But this time it didn't work. Jib tried everything. Nothing worked. Finally he threw himself down on the ground and kicked his feet.

The drumbies turned their heads and watched. They watched Jib for a long time. They rolled their big, soft eyes. They watched a bird flying by. They watched Jib some more. Then Drat-you said something. It sounded like "M-M-M-M-umm," but it meant something like "Shall we?" The drumbie named Star said, "M-M-M-M-oosh." There is no word for "yes" in drumbie language, but "M-M-M-M-oosh" is as close as you can get. Then the two drumbies started off around the field.

At the last field Jib pulled out two more handfuls of hair. He threw himself on the ground and kicked until he wore a hole in his left boot. He asked nicely—and he yelled—and he screamed. At last he sat down in the grass and cried. The drumbies watched him cry and blinked their big, soft eyes. Then they began to plow the field.

It was late when the plowing was finally finished. The sun had gone down, and dark shadows were creeping across the fields. Jib was tired. He had never been so tired in his whole life. He led the drumbies back to the shed in the backyard. He didn't sing to them. He didn't tell them good night. He threw down one armful of hay and said, "Star." He threw down another and said, "Drat-you!" He went out and slammed the door.

Brindle and Trinket and Nipper were in the kitchen when Jib came in. They all looked at him. They looked at his dirty clothes and the hole in his left boot. They looked at his hair and the places where it wasn't anymore. They looked at his storm-cloud face and lightning eyes. They didn't say anything. But they all thought, Drumbies.

That night Jib didn't sit in the parlor and read a drumbie-man story. Instead, soon after dinner was over he said, "Well, I guess I'll turn in early to-night."

"Good idea," Brindle said. "A good night's rest is just what you need."

Trinket looked up from her schoolbooks. "Good night, Father," she said. "Get a good night's rest."

Nipper was lying on the floor with his head on Squeak's fat middle. "Good night's rest, Father," he called.

Jib got slowly to his feet. "Rest," he said, in a slow, shaky voice. "Yes. Rest." He walked very slowly out of the kitchen and up the stairs.

Brindle and Trinket and Nipper watched him go. As soon as he was gone Nipper jumped up.

"What happened?" he asked Brindle. "What happened with the drumbies?"

"I'm not sure," Brindle said. "But whatever it was, it wasn't good."

"Worse than usual?" Trinket asked.

Brindle sighed. "I'm afraid so," she said.

Trinket went back to her books, and Nipper flopped down on the floor again beside Squeak. But after a minute he sat up. He was grinning.

"Well, no more drumbie-man books, I guess."

Trinket giggled. "No more drumbie-man songs."

"And boots," Nipper said. "Did you see his boots? I'll bet we don't hear about drumbie-men ever again. What do you bet?"

"Oh, I don't know," Brindle said. "Don't you remember last year?"

"But last year wasn't as bad," Trinket said.

"Not nearly as bad," Nipper said.

"Well, you're right," Brindle said. "It wasn't as bad. But it wasn't good. Last year it took him two weeks to start in again about drumbies. This year it might take him three."

Brindle tipped her head to one side and thought for a minute. "Yes," she said. "Just about three weeks, I think."

Brindle wasn't quite right. That year it was a whole month before Jib went into the parlor after dinner and sat down in his big chair with a book about drumbie-men.

And it was at least a week more before he began to cross off the days until the next spring plowing.

6. The Little Yellow Quen

One day Nipper was sitting at the kitchen table painting a picture of a goose. It was a goose that he'd read about in a storybook. The goose in Nipper's picture was very big. It had to be big because the story was a STOMPER story, and the goose was a STOMPER goose. There was also an egg in the picture, and it was BIG too. Nipper's picture used up a lot of paper. It also used up a lot of gold paint.

Brindle was sitting in the kitchen too. She was mending some socks. Now and then she hummed a little tune.

All of a sudden Brindle stopped humming. "Do you hear that?" she said.

"Hmmm?" Nipper said. He was busy making the egg bigger and more golden.

"Shh!" Brindle said. "I think I hear something in the garden."

She put down her mending and went to the window. Nipper went on painting.

"I knew it," Brindle said. "I knew it. That little yellow quark of yours is in the garden again."

Nipper knew which quark his mother meant. He had found the little yellow quark in the forest when it was just a quickie.

Baby quarks are called quickies.

The little quickie had looked hungry and lonely. So Nipper brought it home and put it in the pen with the other quarks. But that had been a long time ago.

"It's not my quark," he said. "Just because I found it doesn't make it mine."

"Well, yours or not, it's a real pest. How in the world does it get out of the pen? The other quarks don't get out. Every day I shut it back up, and every day it gets out and scratches up my garden."

Nipper's mother ran outside and the door slammed shut behind her. Nipper went on painting. After a while, the door slammed open and his mother came back in.

"Come help me, Nipper," she said. "I can't catch that silly quark."

Nipper sighed. He put down his brush and followed his mother outside. In the garden the little yellow quark was happily scratching up seedlings with its big quark feet.

All quarks are little, and all quarks have big feet. But the little yellow quark was smaller than most, and its feet were bigger.

"Drat!" Brindle said. "Just look at what that stupid quen has done to my garden."

Female quarks are called quens.

"Is it a quen?" Nipper asked. "It still looks pretty much like a quickie to me."

"I know," Brindle said. "But it's old enough to be a quen. It just didn't grow very much. And it's the wrong color. Why isn't it a nice muddy brown like most quarks? It's just a very strange quark. Come on, Nipper. Help me catch it."

Brindle went around the garden one way. Nipper went around the other. Then they crept quietly toward the yellow quark.

When she was close, Brindle jumped at the quark from one side. Nipper jumped at it from the other. The little quark let out a loud squawk and flew straight up in the air. Brindle grabbed Nipper, and Nipper grabbed Brindle. Nipper's head banged Brindle's nose, and Brindle stepped on Nipper's toes.

Brindle sat down on a cabbage and said, "OUCH!" and rubbed her nose.

Nipper sat on a squash and said, "OUCH!" and rubbed his toes. While they were saying OUCH! the little yellow quark was running around the garden saying, "SQUAWK! SQUAWK! SQUAWK!" Now and then it stepped on seedlings and knocked over bean poles.

"That does it!" Brindle said. "Tomorrow we're going to have quark soup. YELLOW quark soup." Then she got up and began to chase the quark again.

Ten minutes later the little yellow quen was caught. Ten minutes of bumped noses and smashed toes and squashed seedlings and broken bean poles. But at last the quark was caught and shut up in a box. Brindle went back to the kitchen to finish her socks.

Nipper sat down on the ground and rubbed his toes. While he rubbed his toes he watched the quark in the box.

"It serves you right," he said at first.

Inside the box the little yellow quen turned slowly around in circles. It didn't look very smart, but, then, quarks never look very smart. Nipper wondered if it knew that he had saved its life when it was a little lost quickie.

It didn't look very happy either. Nipper wondered if it knew that it would soon be in the soup.

"Poor old stupid quark," he said. The quark turned its head to one side and looked at him. Then it hid its head under its wing.

"Poor little yellow quen," Nipper said. Then he got up and went into the kitchen.

Brindle had finished mending the socks and was starting dinner.

"Mother," Nipper said, "maybe you shouldn't make that little yellow quen into soup."

"Why not?" Brindle asked.

"Well," Nipper said, "it's so little it won't make very much. Maybe you ought to make soup out of a big old quock."

Male quarks are called quocks.

"It will make a little soup," Brindle said. "A little soup is better than no soup. Better than no soup and a scratched-up garden." Brindle rubbed her nose. "Not to mention smashed toes and noses," she said.

"But it's such a strange little quark," Nipper said. "It's almost as small as a quickie, and it's such a funny color. Quarks aren't supposed to be yellow. Don't you think it might make funny-tasting soup?"

"Perhaps," Brindle said. "But funny or not, that quark goes in the pot tomorrow." She stopped peeling potatoes and looked at Nipper. "Why don't you want me to make soup tomorrow?" she asked. "You always like quark soup."

"I know," Nipper said. "I was just . . . wondering."

Brindle smiled. "All right. Everybody wonders about things now and then. But while you're wondering, would you please take your paints off the table so we can have dinner?"

So Nipper took his picture and his paints off the table and took them up to his room. First he put away his paints, and then he looked for a place to hang his picture. While he was looking, he happened to look out of the window. Down by the garden he could see a big brown box. He looked at the box for a while, and then he looked at his picture. Then he looked back at the box.

"Hmmm!" Nipper said.

The next morning Trinket went out to feed the quarks and gather the eggs. On her way back to the house, she stopped to feed the quark in the box. The strange little yellow quen was sitting in the corner of the box with its head under its wing. When Trinket put some grain in the box, it jumped up and began to eat. In the corner of the box there was an egg.

Trinket looked at the egg. She got down on her knees and looked at it more carefully. Next, she put her nose near the box and looked at the egg even more closely. Then she jumped up and ran into the house.

"Mother! Father! Come quick!" Trinket called as she ran into the kitchen. There was no one there. Trinket ran to the stairs. "Mother! Father! Come quick!" she called up the stairs. Nobody answered. Then she heard voices in the parlor.

Trinket ran into the parlor. "Mother! Father! Come—" Trinket was saying—and then she stopped. Sure enough, Jib and Brindle were both there, but company was there too. The company was Verbena Drone.

Trinket knew Mistress Verbena Drone. All the Tiddler folk knew Verbena Drone. Verbena and her husband, Dinky Drone, had a shop in the village. It was a hat shop.

Dinky Drone made the hats. Tiddlers came from miles around to buy his hats. He made boaters and bonnets and bowlers and berets and beanies. He also made pillboxes and porkpies. Dinky Drone was a famous hatmaker.

People also came from miles around to listen to Verbena. Verbena was a famous talker.

"Well, Trinket," Brindle said. "Can't you say good morning to our visitor? Can't you wish Mistress Drone a nice Tuesday morning?"

It had to be Tuesday morning, or else Thursday. On Tuesdays and Thursdays Verbena Drone went visiting. On other days she stayed in the shop and talked to the people who came in. On Mondays, Wednesdays, and Fridays, Verbena talked about the people she visited on Tuesdays and Thursdays. Some people called Verbena the town newspaper. Other people called her the town blabbermouth.

"Excuse me," Trinket said. She curtsied to Verbena Drone. "Good morning, Mistress Drone."

"Good morning, Trinket," Verbena Drone said. Her eyes had gone bright and burny. Her ears wiggled. "You seem a bit excited. Has something happened?"

Trinket was excited. She just had to tell her mother and father about what she had seen. She didn't think about keeping it a secret. She didn't think about what happened to secrets when Verbena heard them.

"Mother! Father! Come quick!" she said. "That little yellow quen has laid a golden egg."

Brindle smiled. "Trinket has a big imagination."

Jib chuckled. "I think Trinket is playing a joke."

Trinket got angry. "It's not imagination. And it's not a joke. It's a golden egg. I saw it."

Verbena Drone put down her teacup and stood up. Her eyes were even brighter, and her ears wiggled harder. "My dear child," she said, "where is the golden egg? MAY I SEE IT?"

Trinket looked at her father and mother. Jib was frowning. Brindle was shaking her head. "Well," Trinket said, "well, I don't know—"

She didn't have time to say any more. Mistress Drone grabbed her and dragged her out the back door. Jib and Brindle got up and came too.

A minute later, Jib and Brindle and Trinket and Mistress Verbena Drone were in the backyard. They were all on their hands and knees by the big brown box. In the box the little yellow quen was still scratching and eating. In the corner of the box was a GOLDEN EGG.

When she saw the egg, Brindle said, "Land-o'-livin'!"

Jib said, "Great jumping jack-o'-lanterns."

"Excuse me, folks," Verbena Drone said. "I must be on my way." She started off down the road as fast as she could go.

Jib jumped up too. "Verbena!" he called. "Please don't say anything about . . ."

Verbena kept going.

"I mean," Jib shouted, "don't tell everybody about . . ."

Verbena walked faster.

Jib took a deep breath. "Keep your mouth shut for once," he yelled. But it was too late. Verbena was already leaning over the Daws' front gate, talking to Fancie Daw. And half an hour later, most of the village was in the Tooleys' backyard.

Nearly everybody was there. There were farmers like the Daws and the Tattles. And shopkeepers like the Barleys and the Drones. Julep Quaff from the tavern was there, along with his best customer, Toper Careen. Mistress Muggins, the mayor, was there also. Even Bluster Swag, the drumbie-man, who was usually out in the wild woods, had stopped by with his wife, Phobia.

Lots of boys and girls were there too. Tuck Barley was there and Dimity Daw, and lots of Dimity's little brothers and sisters, and Petal Swag and her big brother, Jingo, and, of course, the Tattle twins, Dollop and Duffle.

All the boys and girls were busy asking questions about the golden egg. Trinket was busy answering questions about how she had seen it first. Nipper was there too. Nipper was busy not saying anything.

All of the Tooleys' visitors were taking turns getting down on their hands and knees to peek into the brown box. Most of them wanted only to look at the golden egg and the strange little yellow quen. But Bluster Swag wanted to trade a team of drumbies for the golden egg. Jib was busy talking to Bluster.

And Prism Spangle, who owned the jewelry shop, wanted to trade a diamond ring for the little yellow quen. Brindle was busy talking to Prism.

But then Spoot Tattle started saying that the little yellow quen belonged to him.

Spoot Tattle was the Tooleys' neighbor. Just like his sons, the terrible Tattle twins, Spoot's middle name was Trouble. When Spoot saw something he really wanted, he went after it any way he could. Now he was going after the little yellow quen by saying it was his. He also said the Tooleys had stolen it.

"Yes, sir!" Spoot was telling everybody. "Had me a little yellow quen like that this spring. Prettiest little thing you ever saw. But then one day it was gone. Now I guess I know where it went. It's mine, and I can prove it. Come here, boy."

Spoot Tattle grabbed at his twins and caught one of them. "You remember that little yellow quen, don't you, boy?"

"I remember," the twin squealed.

"And what happened to it?" Spoot yelled.

"You threw it out, Pa," the twin said, "because it was too little."

"No!" Spoot bellowed. "No, I didn't!" He grinned at all the people. "Caught the wrong twin," he said. "This one is Duffle. He's the dumb one. Can't remember a thing."

"I'm Dollop," the twin whimpered.

Spoot whacked Dollop and dropped him. Then he caught Duffle.

"What happened to my little yellow quen, boy?" he yelled.

"I don't know, Pa," the twin said. "Did somebody steal it?"

"Right!" Spoot shouted. "Somebody stole it. And now we know who. Jib Tooley, I want my little quen back and my golden egg, too."

Everybody began to shout and argue. Some people thought the quen was the Tooleys', and some thought it was the Tattles'. Everybody shouted and yelled. Everyone except Mistress Muggins and Nipper.

Mistress Muggins was quiet because she was busy deciding things. Nipper was quiet for his own reasons.

At last, the mayor began to thump the ground with her walking stick. She thumped and thumped until people stopped yelling and waving their arms. One by one, they stopped yelling and looked at Mistress Muggins.

"Your mayor," she said, "has decided. The little

yellow quen will stay with Jib Tooley. But Spoot Tattle may have the egg."

Nobody was happy. Jib said, "But what if it never lays another golden egg?"

And Spoot said, "What if it lays a hundred more golden eggs?"

But the mayor would only nod her head and thump her stick. So at last Spoot Tattle stomped over to the brown box. He reached in and grabbed the golden egg. Then he started off toward the gate. Everyone stood on tiptoe to see the shiny golden egg in the middle of Spoot's dirty brown hand.

Just then someone yelled, "Hey there, Spoot. Lemme see that egg."

It was Toper Careen. Toper was the champion ale-drinker of Tiddletown. Sometimes Toper drank so much ale that he walked funny. He walked with a wobble and tripped over his own toes. That particular morning Toper had drunk quite a lot of ale.

"Lemme see that egg," Toper yelled again and started toward Spoot. First he took two fast steps. Then he tripped over his own toes and took two faster steps. Next he waved both arms in the air and ran headfirst into the middle of Spoot Tattle.

"UUMMPH!" Spoot said and sat down HARD. The golden egg flew straight up in the air. When it came down, it landed on top of Spoot's bald head.

SPLAT!

In the middle of Spoot Tattle's head was a little yellow yolk. Around the yolk was some runny white. And just over Spoot's eyebrows were a few pieces of shiny gold eggshell.

Everything got very quiet. Then somebody yelled, "A trick!"

"Yes," some other people said. "A trick. A cheat. Jib Tooley painted the egg. Jib was trying to cheat people."

Everyone looked at Jib.

Mistress Muggins thumped her stick. "Jib Tooley?" she asked.

"No!" Jib was shaking his head. "I didn't . . . I don't know . . . I did not paint that egg!"

Everyone stared at Jib. They all stared and frowned and shook their heads.

"I DID NOT PAINT THAT EGG," Jib said again.

For a long moment nobody said anything.

Finally a little voice said, "I did."

The voice was Nipper's. Everyone looked at him. Nipper put his left hand into his left pocket and pulled out a paint brush. Then he put his right hand into his right pocket and pulled out a jar of gold paint.

"I did it," he said.

Mistress Muggins thumped her stick. When it got quiet, she asked an important question.

"WHY?"

"Because," Nipper said, "because I kind of like that little yellow quen. I didn't want her in the soup."

"I see," Mistress Muggins said.

Everyone looked at Mistress Muggins. They watched her as she tipped her head to the right. Then she tipped her head to the left. Then she thumped on the ground with her walking stick and said, "I see" again. "I see, and I have decided. I have decided that cheating people is a BAD reason to paint an egg. But saving a nice little yellow quen is a GOOD reason to paint an egg. The verdict is . . . NOT GUILTY FOR GOOD REASONS!"

Everybody cheered loudly. Everybody, that is, except Spoot Tattle.

Spoot didn't cheer at all. Maybe he would have if he hadn't been so busy getting egg off his face.

But then again, maybe not.

7. A Doll for Dimity

"Isn't it beautiful? Isn't it just the most beautiful thing you've ever seen in your whole life?"

Dimity Daw pressed her little round nose against the window and sighed. She sighed so hard the window glass got foggy.

Trinket and Dimity were standing in front of the Tiddletown toy shop. The shop window was full of toys, but Dimity was looking at just one—a doll. The doll had pink cheeks and black eyes and a blue polka-dot dress. It was a nice doll, but nothing special.

"Is it really?" Trinket asked. "I mean, THE most beautiful thing you've ever seen in your whole life?"

Dimity didn't answer. She was busy fogging up the window with big sighs. Trinket watched her and wondered.

"Dimity," she asked, "have you ever had a doll?" She had to ask it twice before Dimity stopped sighing and answered.

"Yes," she said. "I've had two of them. But Bobbin broke one, and Vanilla lost the other one in the forest. And now Mama says I don't need another. She says I have plenty of real live dolls to play with."

"Well, I guess that's true, isn't it?" Trinket said. "They certainly are alive, and there's certainly a lot of them."

Dimity Daw had lots of little brothers and sisters. There were Bobbin and Vanilla and Tansy and Doily and Jot and Whit and Iota and some others whose names Trinket couldn't remember.

Dimity sighed again. "I guess so," she said. "Real live dolls that cry and scream and fight with each other and get into your things and tell on you if you whack them. I want a doll that does only what I pretend it's doing. And the rest of the time it sits still and looks beautiful. I want a real doll."

Trinket nodded. She saw what Dimity meant. Poor Dimity. Trinket wished Dimity could have a real doll. She wished . . .

"Wait a minute!" Trinket said. "WAIT—A—MINUTE!"

"All right," Dimity said. "I'm waiting. What are we waiting for?"

"For me to finish having an IDEA. For me to finish figuring something out."

Dimity waited, and after a minute Trinket said, "Yes, I'll do it! I'm going to do it!"

Dimity sighed. "Do what?" she asked patiently. Dimity Daw was a patient person. People who have little brothers and sisters learn to be patient.

"Come on," Trinket said. "We're going to go for a long walk, and on the way I'm going to tell you something. I'm going to tell you . . ." Trinket stopped and thought for a moment. Then she nodded her head. "Yes! I'm going to tell you a story. Come on, Dimity. Hurry!"

A little later Trinket and Dimity were still hurrying, and Dimity was still being patient. They were going somewhere in the deep woods, but Dimity still didn't know where or even why. Trinket had started to tell a story, but she hadn't gotten very far.

"And so then this girl—" Trinket was saying.

Dimity jumped over a pine cone and ran to catch up. "What girl?" she asked.

"This girl I'm telling you about. This girl was going for a walk in the forest. She was thinking about other things and not noticing where she was. All at once, she saw that she was in STOMPER country."

"Ohh!" Dimity said. "Ohh, dear!" She knew that it was bad and dangerous to go into the STOMPER part of the forest. She was surprised that Trinket—that is, she was surprised that the girl in the story—would do such a thing.

"Yes," Trinket said, "she didn't mean to do it, but there she was. In STOMPER country. And then, all of a sudden, she knew where she was. She was very near a place where there was an old hut. It was a STOMPER woodsman's hut."

Dimity looked shocked. "You mean, you . . . you mean this girl had been to that place before?"

"Just once," Trinket said. "Just once and it wasn't her fault that time, either. That time she'd followed her little brother to keep him from getting in trouble."

"Oh," Dimity said, "that's all right, then." Dimity understood about the things you have to do because of little brothers.

"Yes," Trinket said. "And so this girl decided that since she was almost there, she would go a little farther and see the hut again. So she did. BUT—" Trinket stopped hurrying and looked at

Dimity with big eyes. "BUT, when she was looking around inside the hut, she suddenly heard something."

"WHAT?" Dimity squealed. "What did you . . . I mean, what did she hear?"

"She heard," Trinket said, "somebody talking."

"Goodness gracious," Dimity said.

Trinket rolled her eyes and nodded. "That's just what she thought. Goodness gracious, the girl thought. Who could it be? So then this girl peeked out through a crack in the wall and . . ."—Trinket made her eyes even bigger— "And . . . DO YOU KNOW WHAT SHE SAW?"

"NO!" Dimity whispered. "What did she see?"

"She saw a little STOMPER girl coming right toward the hut, pulling a wagon."

"Only one little girl?" Dimity asked. "But who was talking?"

"She was," Trinket said. "She was talking to what was in the wagon. The little STOMPER girl's wagon was full of . . . Can you guess what it was full of, Dimity?"

"No," Dimity said. "I can't guess. What was it full of?"

"It was full of dolls," Trinket said. "STOMPER

dolls. And the little STOMPER girl pulled her wagon right up to the hut and picked up two of the dolls and opened the door—"

"Oh, oh," Dimity cried.

Dimity was terribly excited. She was so excited she forgot it was just a story. "What did you do?" she said. "What did you do, Trinket? Did you blur her eyes?"

Trinket forgot that it was just a story too. "Yes, I did," she said. "But I didn't know if it would work. Sometimes it doesn't with little STOMPERS."

"I know," Dimity whispered.

"So I hid," Trinket said. "I blurred, and I hid too, just in case. There is an old iron stove in the hut, and I hid behind it. And the little STOMPER girl came right into the hut. She put down her dolls and went back out and got some more. There were lots of dolls. Seven or eight of them, and they were all very big. Some of them were baby dolls, and some of them were little girl and boy dolls. But they were all very big. Even the baby dolls were as tall as . . . as tall as Mistress Muggins in her biggest hat."

"Oh, my," Dimity's voice had faded away to almost nothing.

"So then," Trinket said, "she started to play house. She pretended to sweep the floor and wash the windows. And now and then she talked to the dolls and put them in different places and made them do different things. And all the dolls had names. Strange names like Mary and Ann and Timmy and Sally and Sweetie and Babykins."

"Mary and Sally," Dimity said. "What funny names."

Trinket nodded. "Next comes the scariest part."

"Oh, no!" Dimity said.

"The scariest," Trinket said, "because then the little STOMPER girl began to pretend she was making dinner."

"The STOVE!" Dimity gasped.

"Yes, the stove. She came right over to the stove and opened it. She pretended to put wood in it and light a fire. And all the time the toes of her great big STOMPER shoes were so close I could almost touch them. And then she went back out to the wagon. When she came back she had dishes and pots and pans. I guess they were STOMPER doll dishes because they were almost small enough for Tiddler folk."

Trinket stopped to catch her breath and Dimity waited, jumping up and down with excitement. "And what happened then?" she asked.

"And then she sat down on the floor and pretended to stir things and chop things. She came back to the stove and put the pots and pans on it. And next she put all the dolls in a circle on the floor. She put the dishes in front of them and pretended to put dinner in the dishes."

Dimity had stopped jumping. Instead, she was smiling happily. "Oh, that's just the way I'd do it too. That's just the way I'd play house if I had all those dolls and pots and pans and dishes."

Trinket frowned. Dimity had forgotten the important part of the story. "And don't forget," Trinket said, "every time she came back to the stove she almost stepped on me."

"I'm not forgetting," Dimity said. "And what happened then?"

"Then the little STOMPER girl pretended that one of the dolls wouldn't eat its supper. It was a girl doll with long brown curly hair and a pretty green dress. 'Sally,' the STOMPER girl kept saying, 'if you don't eat, you are going to get spanked.' And then she spanked the doll named Sally and made it sit in the corner."

"Oh, good!" Dimity said. "I'm glad she spanked it. If I had lots of dolls I'd spank all of them."

Trinket frowned. "Will you be still, Dimity. How am I going to finish my story if you keep talking?"

"All right. I'll be still," Dimity said. "What happened next?"

"Next, the STOMPER girl held the other dolls in her arms and sang to them and told them a story. And then she put them to bed."

"Was there a bed?" Dimity asked.

"Not a real one. But there was some dry grass in the corner. The STOMPER girl put all the dolls—except Sally—down on the grass and sang to them some more. And then she lay down beside them and pretended to go to sleep. And that's when I got away."

"You got away?"

"Yes. While the STOMPER girl's eyes were shut, I tiptoed out from behind the stove and right out the door."

Dimity smiled. "And then you ran home."

"No, I didn't," Trinket said. "Who's telling this story, anyway?"

"You are. What did you do, if you didn't run home?"

"I decided to play a trick on the little STOMPER. I went around the hut until I was just outside where the doll named Sally was sitting. There are lots of cracks in the walls of the hut. I could see Sally's green dress through a crack. So then I got close to the crack and made a noise like somebody crying."

"TRINKET!" Dimity said. "YOU DIDN'T!"

"Yes, I did. I went BOO-HOO-HOO and SOB-SOB just as loud as I could."

"And then? And then what?" Dimity almost shouted, but Trinket only shook her head.

"I can't tell you the rest. Not yet. I can't tell you the rest until we get there."

"Until we get where?" Dimity squealed.

"To the hut," Trinket said. "We're almost there now. Come on."

Sure enough, in just a few minutes Trinket and Dimity reached the edge of the clearing in the forest. In the middle of the clearing was the old

STOMPER woodsman's hut. Trinket took Dimity's hand. "Come on," she said again.

"No, no," Dimity said. "I can't. I'm afraid."

"Yes, you can," Trinket said. "If you don't, I'll go off without you."

"All right, I'm coming. Don't go without me."

The two girls ran across the clearing through the high grass. The door to the woodsman's hut was wide open. Trinket dropped Dimity's hand and climbed up over the doorsill. Then she reached down and helped Dimity climb up too.

Inside the hut everything was just the way Trinket had said it was. In one corner there was a pile of dry grass. In another there was a huge old iron stove. And—sitting in a third corner was a DOLL. The doll had lots of curly brown hair and a pretty green dress. She had big blue eyes with long eyelashes and a nice smile with pretty white teeth. And if she had been standing up, she would have been quite a bit taller than Mistress Muggins.

"Oh, Trinket," Dimity sighed. "Isn't she beautiful?" She sat down on the floor and stared at the doll and sighed some more.

"Get up from there," Trinket said, "and help me pick her up. We're going to take her home."

"Home?" Dimity squeaked. "To her STOMPER house?"

"Don't be silly," Trinket said. "We're going to take her home to Tiddletown."

"We are?" Dimity said. "How can we?"

"Well," Trinket said, "I'm not sure. But we'll figure out something."

Trinket walked up to Sally on one side and took hold of her. "Come on," she said. "You get the other side. And LIFT!"

They both lifted, and Sally slowly stood right up on her feet. She was twice as tall as Trinket and Dimity.

"Hurrah!" Trinket said. "She's up!"

"She's up!" Dimity said. "Hurrah!"

Then Sally began to lean forward from the hips.

"Look out!" Trinket yelled. "She's bending!"

Trinket and Dimity reached up as high as they could, but it wasn't high enough. Sally went on bending. She leaned farther and farther until the top of her head was on the floor. Then her feet slid backward until she was lying on her face.

"Well," Dimity said, "what do we do now?"

"I don't know," Trinket said. "Let me think."

Trinket walked slowly around the doll. She

lifted one of its arms and put it back down. Then she lifted one of its legs.

"It's not very heavy," she said finally. "Just floppy. I think we'll just have to get under it and carry it on our backs."

A few minutes later, Trinket and Dimity came out of the hut carrying the STOMPER doll on their backs. The top half of Sally was on Trinket's back, and the bottom half was on Dimity's. It worked pretty well, except that Sally's hands and feet hung down and got in the way. Trinket kept tripping over Sally's hands, and Dimity kept tripping over her feet. Before long, Trinket and Dimity were quite tired. But they kept going until they were back in the safe part of the forest.

"My back is hurting," Dimity said finally. "Can we stop and rest now?"

"I'm tired too," Trinket said. "Come on. Let's put her down. Are you ready? Let's lean to the left. Ready, set, LEAN!"

When Trinket and Dimity leaned, Sally rolled off their backs and landed in the soft grass. After they sat her up, they pulled her over against a tree trunk. They smoothed down her green dress and

curly brown hair and folded her hands in her lap. Then they sat down side by side and looked at her.

"What are we going to tell our parents?" Dimity asked suddenly.

"We'll just tell the truth—or most of it, anyway. We'll just say we found her in the forest. The STOMPERS are always dropping things in the forest."

Dimity nodded. "That's true. And we did find her in the forest." After a minute she said, "Oh! You didn't tell me the rest of the story. What happened when you made the crying noise through the crack in the hut?"

"Oh, yes," Trinket said. "At first the little STOMPER girl stopped pretending to sleep and sat up. Then she looked all around. She looked hard at Sally, and her eyes got very big. So then I made the crying noise once more."

Trinket wrinkled up her face and went BOO-HOO-HOO, SOB-SOB again to show how she did it. Then she stopped crying and shook her head sadly.

"What happened?" Dimity asked. "Why are you looking sad?"

"I did it only for a joke," Trinket said. "I didn't

think it would scare the little STOMPER so much. But it did. It scared her so much that she started running around picking up all her dolls and dishes. All her dolls, that is, except Sally. She threw everything into her wagon. And then she ran away with the wagon bouncing and rattling behind her."

"Oh, dear," Dimity said. "Poor little STOMPER." But then suddenly she giggled. "It is kind of funny, though," she said.

Trinket stopped looking so sad. "I know," she said, smiling just a little.

"What did you do then?"

"I went back into the hut and looked around. I looked at poor Sally sitting all alone in the corner. Then I went on home."

"Why did you leave Sally there all alone?" Dimity asked.

"I thought the STOMPER girl might come back for her after she stopped being so scared. It would be wrong to take her if the little STOMPER was going to want her back. But I guess she doesn't, or she would have come for her by now."

"I guess not," Dimity said. "But why wouldn't you tell me the rest of the story until now?"

"Because I thought the girl might have come back and taken her away. I didn't want to tell you we were going to get you a STOMPER doll until I knew she was still there."

"Oh, I see," Dimity said. All of a sudden, her face lit up. "To get ME a STOMPER doll?" she asked. "You mean Sally is mine?"

"If you want her," Trinket said. "I don't think I'd want her. She's too big to carry around, or even to hold on my lap. I'm afraid she's just too big for a doll."

"No, no," Dimity said. "She's not too big. She's perfect."

"Perfect for what? What will you do with her?"

Dimity thought for a moment. "I'll put her in my room, and she'll sit there and look beautiful. And she'll be too big for Bobbin to break or for Vanilla to lose in the forest. And Whit and Jot won't be able to drag her around by the leg, like they did my other dolls."

Dimity sighed happily. "Everyone with little brothers and sisters," she said, "should have a doll that is bigger than Mistress Muggins."

About the Author

Zilpha Keatley Snyder has written many distinguished books for children, including *The Egypt Game, The Headless Cupid,* and *The Witches of Worm,* all Newbery Honor Books and American Library Association Notable Books for Children. She lives in Marin County, California.